W9-AHX-082

EASY READERS

Why We Have Thanksgiving

by Margaret Hillert

Illustrated by Dan Siculan

DEAR CAREGIVER, The *Beginning-to-Read* series is a carefully written collection of classic readers you may remember from your own childhood. Each book features text comprised of common sight words to provide your child ample practice reading the words that appear most frequently in written text. The many additional details in the pictures enhance the story and offer the opportunity for you to help your child expand oral language and develop comprehension.

Begin by reading the story to your child, followed by letting him or her read familiar words and soon your child will be able to read the story independently. At each step of the way, be sure to praise your reader's efforts to build his or her confidence as an independent reader. Discuss the pictures and encourage your child to make connections between the story and his or her own life. At the end of the story, you will find reading activities and a word list that will help your child practice and strengthen beginning reading skills.

Above all, the most important part of the reading experience is to have fun and enjoy it!

Shannon Cannon

Shannon Cannon,
Literacy Consultant

Norwood House Press • P.O. Box 316598 • Chicago, Illinois 60631
For more information about Norwood House Press please visit our website at
www.norwoodhousepress.com or call 866-565-2900.

LIBRARY OF CONGRESS CATALOGING-IN-PUBLICATION DATA
Hillert, Margaret.
 Why we have Thanksgiving / by Margaret Hillert; illustrated by Dan
Siculan. — Rev. and expanded library ed.
   p. cm. — (Beginning-to-read book)
 Summary: An easy-to-read fictional retelling of the journey of the
Pilgrims to America, their struggles during the first year, and celebration
of the first Thanksgiving. Includes reading activities.
 ISBN-13: 978-1-59953-049-9 (library binding : alk. paper)
 ISBN-10: 1-59953-049-X (library binding : alk. paper)
 [1. Thanksgiving Day—Fiction. 2. Pilgrims (New Plymouth Colony)—Fiction.]
 I. Siculan, Dan, ill. II. Title. III. Series: Hillert, Margaret. Beginning
to read series. Easy stories.
 PZ7.H558Whi 2007
 [E]—dc22   2006007892

I want you to go here.
You have to do what I want.
Go here. Go here.

3

We do not want to go there.
We do not like it.
We want to do what we like.

You can not do what you like.
Get in here.
Get in here.
This is the spot for you.

We do not like this.
Oh, we do not like this.
What can we do?
What can we do?

We can go away.
Yes, we can go away.
That is what we can do.
We can go in a boat.
A big, big boat.

Come on. Come on.
Get this on the boat.
We have to have it.
Work, work, work.

Oh, what a big boat!
We will go on it with
Mother and Father.
We will go away on it.

Here we are on the boat.
This is fun.
Away we go.

Away we go.
But where will we go?
What will we see?

Oh, look.
Do you see that?
Will we like it here?

15

Look up, up.
Look at that.
Do you see what I see?
How funny.

Come on.
Run, run, run.
This is fun for us.
Fun for you and me.

I guess Father and Mother
did not like it.
Here we are on a boat.
Now where will we go?

What is this spot?
Is it a good one?
What will we do here?

We have to work.
We have to make a big
house for boys and girls
and mothers and fathers.

Oh, this is good.
Now Father can make
a house for us.
We can help.
See what we can do.

Look out. Look out.
Who is that?
What will he do?
Help! Help!

Why, he wants to help.
What a big help he is.
This is good.

See this come up,
and this,
and this.
It is good to eat.

And here is something
to eat, too.
Something little and red.
Something good.
We can get some for
Mother and Father.

Now, sit down. Sit down.
It is good to have
something to eat.
It is good to have friends.

READING REINFORCEMENT

The following activities support the findings of the National Reading Panel that determined the most effective components for reading instruction are: Phonemic Awareness, Phonics, Vocabulary, Fluency, and Text Comprehension.

Phonemic Awareness: The /w/ sound

Oral Blending: Say the beginning and ending sounds of the following words and ask your child to listen to the sounds and say the whole word:

/w/ + ill = will	/w/ + ing = wing	/w/ + all = wall
/w/ + eek = week	/w/ + ith = with	/w/ + ell = well
/w/ + ould = would	/w/ + alk – walk	/w/ + in = win
/w/ + ash = wash	/w/ + ide = wide	/w/ + ink = wink

Phonics: The letter Ww

1. Demonstrate how to form the letters **W** and **w** for your child.

2. Have your child practice writing **W** and **w** at least three times each.

3. Ask your child to point to the words in the book that begin with the letter **w**.

4. Write down the following words and ask your child to circle the letter **w** in each word:

how	water	wait	swing	flower
who	what	sew	when	sweep
now	work	swim	fewer	went

Vocabulary: Suffix -ful

1. Explain to your child that the suffix -ful means "full of".

2. Say the following words and ask your child add the suffix -ful to each one:

joy + ful = joyful   care + ful = careful   thank + ful = thankful

help + ful = helpful   grate + ful = grateful   truth + ful = truthful

respect + ful = respectful   thought + ful = thoughtful   peace + ful = peaceful

3. Write each word on a separate piece of paper.

4. Read each word aloud for your child.

5. Take turns with your child pointing to a word and describing a time when you were...(...joyful, careful, thankful, etc.)

Fluency: Shared Reading

1. Reread the story to your child at least two more times while your child tracks the print by running a finger under the words as they are read. Ask your child to read the words he or she knows with you.

2. Reread the story taking turns, alternating readers between sentences or pages.

Text Comprehension: Discussion Time

1. Ask your child to retell the sequence of events in the story.

2. To check comprehension, ask your child the following questions:

- What happened to the people who did not obey the king?
- Why did the people go away on the boat?
- What kind of work did the people do when they got to the new place?
- How did the people celebrate with their friends?
- How does your family celebrate Thanksgiving?

WORD LIST

Why We Have Thanksgiving uses the 73 words listed below.
This list can be used to practice reading the words that appear in the text.
You may wish to write the words on index cards and use them to help your
child build automatic word recognition. Regular practice with these words
will enhance your child's fluency in reading connected text.

a	father(s)	I	oh	up
and	for	in	on	us
are	friends	is	one	
at	fun	it	out	want(s)
away	funny			we
		like	red	what
big	get	little	run	where
boat	girls	look		who
boys	go		see	why
but	good	make	sit	will
	guess	me	some	with
		mother(s)	something	work
can			spot	
come	have			
	he	not		yes
did	help	now	that	you
do	here		the	
down	how		there	
	house		this	
eat			to	
			too	

ABOUT THE AUTHOR   Margaret Hillert has written over 80 books for
children who are just learning to read. Her books
have been translated into many different languages and over a million children
throughout the world have read her books. She first started writing poetry as
a child and has continued to write for children and adults throughout her life. A
first grade teacher for 34 years, Margaret is now retired from teaching and lives in
Michigan where she likes to write, take walks in the morning, and care for her three cats.

Photograph by Glenna Washburn

ABOUT THE ADVISER   Shannon Cannon contributed the activities pages that appear in
this book. Shannon serves as a literacy consultant and provides
staff development to help improve reading instruction. She is a frequent presenter at educational
conferences and workshops. Prior to this she worked as an elementary school teacher and as
president of a curriculum publishing company.